My Brother and Me

Text: Taghreed Najjar
Illustrations: Maya Fidawi

CRACKBOOM!

My name is Aloush and I'm the youngest person in my family. But when people call me *the baby*, it makes me mad.

I say to my grandma, "I am Aloush,
I am a person. Please, don't call me *the baby*
anymore." My grandma just laughs and
pats me on the head.

Being the youngest in the family is good and bad at the same time. Sure, everyone in your family spoils you, but when you express your opinion about anything, they just laugh and pat you on the head. They don't take you seriously, just because you're young.

My brother Ramez is much older than me.
He graduated from college and works at
an engineering company. Ramez is my
favorite person in the whole world!
Every day on his way to work he drops me
off at school.

When he goes to the gym to play basketball he takes me with him, and when the game is over, he teaches me how to hold the ball and shoot it through the hoop.

On weekends, he sometimes drives my friend Hamoudeh and me to watch a movie at the mall. He buys us popcorn and soda, and after the film is over he brings us back home.

What I enjoy most is when Ramez lets me watch a soccer game with him and his friends. I shout and cheer with them and feel that I'm grown up too.

But lately Ramez seems different. I don't know why. He spends most of his time in his room talking and laughing on the telephone, and if I come in, he motions to me to leave.

He spends a long time in the bathroom before he leaves the house. He shaves and puts gel on his hair. He changes his hairstyle ten times before he's satisfied, then he puts cologne on his chin and neck.

These days Ramez is always busy. When I ask him to help me with my homework, he smiles and says, "I am busy, Aloush. I have an appointment with someone very important."
"Are you going to the dentist?" I ask.
Ramez laughs and pats me on the head. This makes me so mad that I turn my back to him.

I complain to Baba: "I don't understand why Ramez is always too busy to do things with me."
Baba laughs, "When you're older, you'll understand."

One day I hear Mama ululating—
loo loo loo leeeeeee! "I'm over the
moon! Ramez is getting engaged."
I can feel my world slowly crumble
and fall apart. Ramez is getting
engaged! Who to? And why? And is
he going to move out of the house
and leave me?

Ramez says, "Come here, Aloush. I want to show you a picture of my fiancée." Everyone gathers around Ramez. "What a lovely girl! What's her name? What's her family's name? Where does she live? What's she studying?"

"Her name is Deema and she's a third-year engineering student," Ramez replies.

To be honest, I don't find her sweet or pretty, and decide not to like her. Wasn't she taking my brother Ramez away from me?

Everybody in the house is busy with Ramez's engagement and the *jaha*. Ramez tells me that a *jaha* is when the men of the family visit the bride-to-be's house to formally ask for her hand in marriage. Mama says, "Aloush is too young to go to the engagement ceremony," but Ramez insists I come along with the men. I proudly put on a suit and tie and climb into the car with my father and uncles.

After the *jaha,* Ramez is even busier than before. I don't get to see him at all. He doesn't have any time to take me to the mall with Hamoudeh, or to shoot baskets, or… or… And all because of Deema!

A few days later, Mama says excitedly, "Tomorrow evening Deema's family is coming to dinner. We need to get everything ready." Mama makes a list of all the things she needs from the supermarket and asks me to come with her to help.

When we get back Mama and Grandma start preparing all sorts of dishes—tabbouleh, hummus, spinach-filled pastries, and many others.

"All of this for Miss Deema!" I complain. But no one pays any attention. As I leave the room, Mama says, "Don't forget to wear your best outfit to welcome Deema and her family to our house."

"We were so happy before Ramez met Deema!" I say to myself sadly.

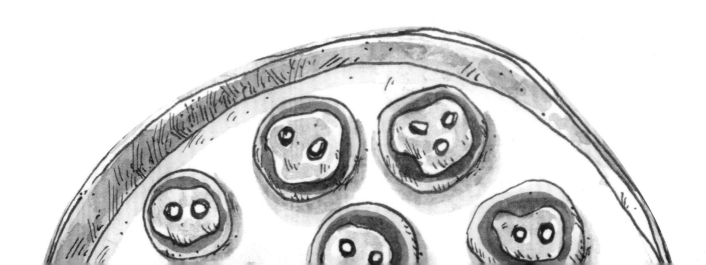

Finally, Deema and her family arrive. The room is abuzz with chatter and laughter but when I come in, everybody stops talking and looks at me in amazement. "Aloush!" Ramez says angrily, "Why are you wearing your dirty soccer uniform? Don't you know we have guests?" Mama exclaims, "Where did you get these clothes from, Aloush?"

"From the laundry basket," I say defiantly. Everybody laughs. Deema says, "No worries, let him wear whatever he likes." But Ramez is furious with me and Mama sends me to my room to change.

The second time Deema visits us, she asks for a glass of water. I tell my mother that I'll bring it. But when I get close to Deema I stumble and spill the glass of water all over her. Deema jumps to her feet. Ramez shouts at me, "Aloush! Look at the mess you made!"

Deema wipes her shirt with a towel Mama gives her and says, "No problem, these things happen. Please, don't be angry at Aloush, Ramez. It was an accident. Right, Aloush?" I look down at my shoes and mumble, "Sorry, I didn't mean to."

My plan to drive Deema away from Ramez wasn't working. That night I toss and turn in bed trying to hatch a new plan. Finally, the perfect idea comes to me and I fall fast asleep.

On Deema's third visit to our house, I give her a gift-wrapped box.
Deema says, "A gift for me from Aloush! What a nice surprise!"
But when Deema opens the box she screams.

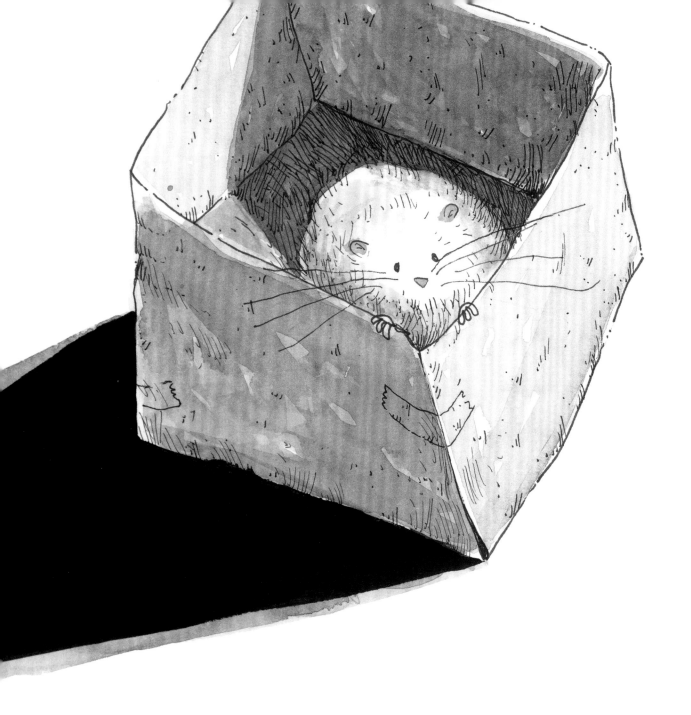

She laughs. "Aloush likes practical jokes! Where did you find the mouse?"
"He's not a mouse," I answer. "He's a hamster and he lives in a cage in my room. Did he scare you?"
"Yes," Deema says, "I was a little bit scared at first, but I love animals. Does your hamster have a name?"
"His name is Nafnoof," I say. Deema thinks for a moment. "It's a strange name for a hamster," she says, "but I like it."

"Aloush, can I help you put your hamster back in his cage?"
I hesitate, but I bring Deema to my room. We put Nafnoof
back in his cage, and we watch him run on his wheel.

After that, I show Deema my collection of toy cars, and after that we play a video game on my computer. That's when Ramez comes looking for Deema. When he sees us engrossed in the game, he says, "Aloush, you've stolen my fiancée!"

"Wait just a minute, Ramez!" I say excitedly. "The game's almost finished."

Ramez laughs. "What do you
think of Deema now, Aloush?"
he asks.
I smile. "Not bad," I say shyly.
Deema hugs me and says,
"Aloush, you're the greatest!
Would you be my little brother?
I've always wanted one."
"Hmm," I say, hugging her.
"I'll think about it."

Instagram

Damdooom_moon12
Weibdeh_Amman

28 likes
alloush_undertaker

دمة
يلا نلعب وحوش وديما مرات

Now, whenever the doorbell rings, Ramez and I race each other to greet Deema. She laughs and says, "Hello to the two handsomest young men in town!"

English Edition: ©2019 CHOUETTE PUBLISHING (1987) INC.
Original Arabic Matha Hasal Li Akhi Ramez?
Original Arabic Text: © Taghreed Najjar, 2016. All Rights Reserved.
Illustrations: © Maya Fidawi, 2016.
Originally published in the Arabic language by Al Salwa Publishers, Amman, Jordan 2016

CrackBoom! Books is an imprint of Chouette Publishing (1987) Inc.

Text: Taghreed Najjar
Illustrations: Maya Fidawi

Chouette Publishing would like to thank the Government of Canada and SODEC
for their financial support.

CRACKBOOM! BOOKS

©2019 Chouette Publishing (1987) Inc.
1001 Lenoir St., Suite B-238
Montreal, Quebec H4C 2Z6 Canada
crackboombooks.com

Printed in China
10 9 8 7 6 5 4 3 2 1   CHO2055 JAN2019